31255000011703

ABOUT THE BANK STREET READY-TO-READ SERIES

Seventy years of educational research and innovative teaching have given the Bank Street College of Education the reputation as America's most trusted name in early childhood education.

Because no two children are exactly alike in their development, we have designed the *Bank Street Ready-to-Read* series in three levels to accommodate the individual stages of reading readiness of children ages four through eight.

○ *Level 1:* GETTING READY TO READ—read-alouds for children who are taking their first steps toward reading.

● *Level 2:* READING TOGETHER—for children who are just beginning to read by themselves but may need a little help.

○ *Level 3:* I CAN READ IT MYSELF—for children who can read independently.

Our three levels make it easy to select the books most appropriate for a child's development and enable him or her to grow with the series step by step. The *Bank Street Ready-to-Read* books also overlap and reinforce each other, further encouraging the reading process.

We feel that making reading fun and enjoyable is the single most important thing that you can do to help children become good readers. And we hope you'll be a part of Bank Street's long tradition of learning through sharing.

The Bank Street College of Education

To my parents, with thanks
for the African experience
—K.M.

"I AM NOT AFRAID!"

A Bantam Little Rooster Book/February 1993

Little Rooster is a trademark of Bantam Books,
a division of Bantam Doubleday Dell Publishing Group, Inc.

Series graphic design by Alex Jay/Studio J

Special thanks to James A. Levine, Betsy Gould,
Diane Arico, and Herb Spiers.

Library of Congress Cataloging-in-Publication Data

Mann, Kenny.
"I am not afraid!" / by Kenny Mann ;
illustrated by Richard Leonard and Alfredo Alcala.
p. cm.—(Bank Street ready-to-read)
"A Byron Preiss book."
"A Bantam Little Rooster book."
Summary: After a visit from a hungry demon,
a boy learns courage from his older brother.
ISBN 0-553-09119-0.—ISBN 0-553-37108-8 (pbk.)
[1. Folklore, Masai.] I. Leonard, Richard, ill.
II. Alcala, Alfredo P., ill.
III. Title. IV. Series.
PZ8.1.M2977Iaam 1993
398.2—dc20
[E]
92-13811 CIP AC

Published simultaneously in the United States and Canada

PRINTED IN THE UNITED STATES OF AMERICA

0 9 8 7 6 5 4 3 2 1

Bank Street Ready-to-Read™

"I Am Not Afraid!"

Based on a Masai tale

by Kenny Mann
Illustrated by Richard Leonard
and Alfredo Alcala

A Byron Preiss Book

A BANTAM LITTLE ROOSTER BOOK
NEW YORK · TORONTO · LONDON · SYDNEY · AUCKLAND

Once there were two brothers.
Tipilit, the older, knew no fear.
Leyo was but a boy.
He was small and meek,
with much to learn
from his brother.

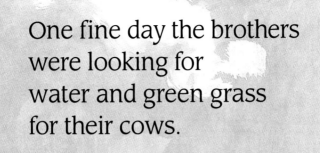

One fine day the brothers
were looking for
water and green grass
for their cows.

They came to a deep river
with green grass all around.
"Let us camp here," said Tipilit.
"I will get some water," said Leyo.

Leyo dipped his gourd
into the river
and filled it with water.
"You are stealing my water!"
roared the river.

Leyo was so afraid,
he fell and spilled the water.
He ran back to his brother.
"The river is angry with me!"
he cried.
"I cannot take any water!"

"You are a coward," said Tipilit.
He picked up the gourd
and filled it with water.

"You are stealing my water!"
roared the river.
"No, oh river," said Tipilit.
"I am taking only what I need,
so I am not afraid."

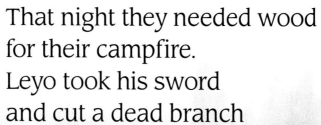

That night they needed wood
for their campfire.
Leyo took his sword
and cut a dead branch
from a tree.

"You are stealing my branches!"
cried the tree.
Leyo was so afraid,
he dropped the branch
and ran back to his brother.

"You are a coward," said Tipilit.
"I will get the wood myself."
Then he took the sword
and cut off a dead branch.

"You are stealing my branches!"
cried the tree.
"No, oh tree," said Tipilit.
"I am taking only dead branches,
so I am not afraid."

The brothers made a fire
with the branches.
They ate their food.
Then, under the full moon,
they fell asleep.

While they were sleeping,
a demon came to their camp.
This demon had nine heads
and one very big toe.

He had one red eye
that glowed in the dark.
And he was very hungry.

The demon was about to steal
the boys' food
when Tipilit woke up.
Quickly, the demon hid
near the dying fire.
Only his red eye glowed
in the dark.

"The fire is almost out,"
Tipilit told Leyo.
"Make a new one."
Leyo put branches on the fire.
He reached for
a chunk of coal.
But it was the demon's eye!

Quickly, the demon seized Leyo.
The boy was so frightened,
he could not move.

"Oh brother, help me!"
he cried.
But it was too late.
The demon ate Leyo
in one gulp.

Tipilit chased the demon.
"I am not afraid of you!"
he shouted.
He drew his sword
and chopped off
two of the demon's heads.

The demon's red eye
grew dim and cold.

Tipilit raised his sword again.
Chop!
Off came the demon's big toe.
The demon fell to the ground,
and out crawled Leyo.
He was still alive and
all in one piece.

"My brother," said Leyo,
"you are a brave man.
I, too, wish to be brave."

25

Tipilit smiled
in the pale light of dawn.
"Then go and take water
from the river," he said.
"But this time show no fear."

Leyo dipped his gourd
into the river.
"You are stealing my water!"
roared the river.
"No, oh river!"
shouted Leyo.
"I am taking only what I need.
And I am no longer afraid."

Next, Leyo cut branches
from a tree.
"You are stealing my branches!"
cried the tree.
"No, oh tree!"
shouted Leyo.
"I am taking only dead branches.
And I am no longer afraid."

29

That night the two brothers
rested near their fire.
They sang about the beautiful place
they had found
for their cows.
Their voices rose up
into the starry sky.

The spirits of the trees
and the river rested, too.
Leyo knew they would trouble
him no more.

31

Author's Note

"I Am Not Afraid!" is a Masai folktale. The Masai live in Kenya and Tanzania. They keep many cattle and move from place to place, always searching for fresh grazing grounds.

Masai boys belong to special groups based on their ages. They belong to these groups for their entire lives. This story shows how an older brother acts as a role model for his younger brother, who obeys him and regards him with great respect.

Kenny Mann was born and raised in Kenya. Part of her life was spent on a farm in Masailand. She graduated from the University of East Africa in Nairobi and lived in England and Germany for many years before moving to the United States. She is a writer and journalist who currently works with the Publications Group at Bank Street College. Kenny lives in Sag Harbor, New York, with her daughter, Sophie.

Richard Leonard is the illustrator of many book jackets as well as the Reflections of a Black Cowboy series. He lives in New York City.

Alfredo Alcala is a veteran comic-book and graphic artist whose credits include *Batman* and countless others. He lives in California.